Robinson Crusoe

RETOLD BY PAULINE FRANCIS

Evans

EVANS BROTHERS LIMITED

First published in this edition in 2010
by Evans Brothers Limited
2A Portman Mansions
Chiltern Street
London Wl U 6NR

Cover design and illustration by Emil Dacanay, D.R. Ink
Inside illustrations by Neil Reed

Printed in China by Midas Printing International Ltd.

British Library Cataloguing in Publication data
A cataloguing record for this book is available from the British Library.

ISBN 9780237540968

Robinson Crusoe

Introduction

Daniel Defoe was born in London in 1660 and lived through the Plague and the Great Fire of London of 1666. He travelled for many years in Europe, before and after his marriage; but he was bankrupt a few years later.

Daniel Defoe had many jobs. At one time, he wrote a newspaper called *The Review*; at another, he was a spy! He also wrote many books and magazines about history, geography and travel.

He did not write stories until he was almost sixty years old. *Robinson Crusoe* was his first novel and it was successful from the first day that it was published in 1719. Defoe's story was based on the story of Alexander Selkirk, a Scotsman who was left on a desert island for five years after a quarrel with the captain of his ship. Selkirk's story, *The Englishman*, was published in 1713.

Daniel Defoe's other novels include *A Journal of the Plague Years* and *Moll Flanders*. He died in 1731, at the age of seventy-one, and is buried in London.

CHAPTER ONE

Shipwreck!

I ran away from my home in England to go to sea when I was eighteen years old. Exactly nine years later, I set out on another adventure when some dear friends asked me to help them trade in Africa. I left my tobacco farm in Brazil and sailed with them. We passed the mouth of the great Amazon river and the great Orinoco river in the south Caribbean sea. Then all our troubles began.

A fierce storm began to blow and for twelve days we waited for the waves to swallow us up. One man died of fever and two fell overboard.

At last, the wind died down.

"We must repair the ship," said our captain, "she will not reach Africa now. We'll make for one of the Caribbean islands."

But on the way, a second storm struck. The wind carried us far away from the coast, and we were terrified of what might happen.

"What if the wind takes us to a land where cannibals might eat us!" I cried.

As we all trembled in terror at these horrible thoughts, one of the men cried, "Land - ho!" and we ran from our cabins to look. At the same moment, the ship struck a sandbank, about two miles from land.

"Now they can come and kill us if the sea does not!" I cried.

"The ship will not hold much longer in this wind!" the captain shouted. "Let down one of the boats."

We managed to throw one of the boats into the water and we climbed on board. There were eleven of us, at the mercy of God and the wild sea.

"We cannot stay afloat for long in such high seas," I thought, "we shall all be drowned."

We pulled hard on the oars and made for land, like men going to an execution. As we came nearer, the land looked more frightening than the sea.

"Even if we reach the shore, the waves or the rocks will smash us to pieces!" I shrieked to my friends.

We rowed on for another half a mile. Then, suddenly, a wave as high as a mountain rolled up behind us. It lifted us into the air for a moment, then threw us out of the boat and into the wild sea.

I sank under the water. I was a good swimmer, but the water was so rough that I could not get my breath. But that same wave carried me forward towards the shore, and left me there, half dead. I struggled to my feet and started to walk forward. Soon, a second wave, as high as a hill, came after me, and buried me twenty or thirty feet. I could not avoid it. I held my breath and swam towards

the land. When my lungs were almost bursting, I put my
feet down and felt the sand under them. As soon as the
wave had gone, I ran as fast as I could, afraid that another
wave would pull me back.

I could not get away from that angry sea. Twice more, it lifted me up and threw me against large rocks. They bruised my head and side; but I held onto the rocks whenever the waves broke over my head. Then I ran. In this way, I was able to climb the cliffs. At last, I lay on the grass at the top and was violently sick.

I looked out to sea, hoping to catch sight of my fellow sailors; but I only glimpsed three hats and two shoes floating on the water. My ship was so far out to sea that I wondered how I had ever got to dry land.

I ran up and down the shore.

"Help! Help me!" I shouted in terror. "I have no food, no house, no clothes! The wild animals will eat me! Help!"

Although I was tired and faint, I kept watch until night fell; but no one came. At last, I pulled myself up into a tree, away from danger, and slept very well even though it rained all night.

But I was completely alone.

CHAPTER TWO

My fortress

In the morning, to my great surprise, I saw that the ship had floated in with the high tide and was much nearer the island. The sea was very calm. I had only one thought in my mind. "If we had waited for the storm to die down, we could *all* have reached this shore." I sat and wept for my friends.

I went down to the seashore.

"I shall have to swim out to the ship," I thought. "I must go as soon as possible before she breaks up."

I reached the ship easily. But how could I get on board? I swam around until I saw a rope hanging down. I managed to reach it and I swung onto the deck. Luckily, all the ship's food was still dry – biscuits, bread, flour, rice and some dried meats.

There was so much to take with me that I made a small raft from the ship's mast and the sails.

As I was loading my raft, two cats came to watch and I decided to take them with me. At last, I pushed away. I heard a loud splash behind me and I saw the captain's dog in the water. The faithful creature swam after me all the way to the shore.

I went back to the ship many times after that. I found clothes, a hammock, candles, rope, a gun and gunpowder for it, and, most important of all, the carpenter's box of tools. Then, one night the wind blew hard, and in the morning, I saw that the ship had disappeared.

I had now been on land for twelve days.

"I must find out where I am," I told myself. "Perhaps I can walk inland and find people to help me."

I saw a steep hill about a mile away. I climbed to the top and looked all around me. Tears sprang to my eyes.

"I am on an island!" I wept. "How will I ever get away?"

But I did not have much time to feel sorry for myself.

"I cannot live in a tree much longer," I thought. "I shall make myself a little fortress, away from the hot sun and prowling animals. I must be away from the water's edge, but close enough to the sea to keep a watch for passing ships."

I chose the place for my home on a small hill. I made a tent from the ship's sail, and put it on a ledge under a rock. I cut up the ship's mast, and placed a half-circle of posts in front of my tent. Then I began to work my way into the rock of the hill to make a cellar for my house. Instead of a door to my fortress, I made a ladder, which I pulled up whenever I went inside.

Time passed very quickly, so quickly that I began to keep a record of the days. I had no pen or paper or ink, so I put a large post on the shore where I had landed and made a mark for every day that passed. At the top of the post, I nailed a cross and carved these words:

I came on shore here the 30th of September 1659

How I wished my dog could talk to me! I was sick and tired of hearing my own voice. But he was a great comfort to me as I worked. I had never used tools before, yet I found that, with time and patience, I could make what I wanted. I made a table and chairs and shelves where I laid out all my belongings. I knocked nails into the wall of rock to hang up my guns and anything else that would hang up.

It was a great pleasure to me to see all my things in such good order. More importantly, this work stopped me thinking about the dangers I faced every day. I had enough to eat. Every day, I went into the woods and shot goats and birds.

I became unhappy when dark fell at seven o'clock every night. When I was trying to rest or sleep, terrible thoughts came into my mind. What would become of me? What if wild animals or wild men attacked me?

I hardly dared to think of the future.

CHAPTER THREE

Earthquake and hurricane

A few months later, in the middle of April, I was working at the entrance to my cave when I heard an enormous roar. Stones started to fall on my head.

"Perhaps I have dug too deep into the hillside, and weakened it," I thought. "Am I going to be buried alive after all my hard work?"

I rushed to my ladder and climbed down to the ground. But my troubles were not over. The earth was shaking under my feet, and it continued to shake for at least thirty minutes. Huge rocks fell into the sea with a dreadful noise, and then the sea started to bubble.

I felt sick with terror and with the movement of the earth. I feared for my life. After the third shock, I sat on the ground, not knowing what to do. I cried, "Lord have mercy upon me!" from time to time; but when the earthquake was over, I thought no more about God.

Then the wind began to blow hard, until the sea was covered in froth and the water rose over the trees. In less than half an hour, the wind had become a hurricane and uprooted some of the trees. It began to rain so hard that I went into my tent; but the rain was so violent that I finally went into my cave, terrified that it would fall down on my head.

In the cave, I had a new problem. It was filling up with rain water. I set to work at once and cut a hole in my wall to let out the water. I sat in my cave for two days and nights. The fear of being buried alive stopped me from sleeping well.

Life was just returning to normal after these terrors, when I fell ill. I started to shiver as if it was winter, then I had strong pains in my head and a fever. I was very frightened. After a week, I forced myself to pick up my gun and go hunting because I had very little food. I killed a she-goat and managed to cook some of it. But the effort was too great for me. The next day, I was ill again.

I was so weak by the end of the day that I could not even stand up to fetch some water. I lay in my hammock and cried out, "Lord have mercy upon me!" until I fell asleep. But this sleep brought me the worst nightmare I have ever had.

I dreamed that I was sitting outside. A man came down to the ground out of a great black cloud, in a bright flame of fire. His face was terrifying as he moved towards me, carrying a long spear. Then he spoke to me.

"You have not said you are sorry for the wrong things you have done in your life. Now you shall die."

He lifted up his spear, ready to kill me, and I woke up.

I recovered very slowly from my illness. The dream had a great effect on me. I thought a great deal about my past life, and for the first time in many years, I opened a Bible from the tea chest and read in amazement on the page I had found:

"Call on me in the day of trouble..."

These words had a great effect on me. When I went to bed that night, I did what I had never done in my life. I knelt down and prayed to God. At first, I thought that God might save me from this lonely life on Despair Island. But, as I read and thought, I knew that God was there to save me from the guilt I felt about running away from my family.

I felt more at peace than I had ever felt since I had arrived on my island.

CHAPTER FOUR

Footprint in the sand

When I was fully well again, I decided to make my life as interesting and as comfortable as I could.

"I have been here for almost a year already," I sighed to myself, "and I have seen no other human being, or ship. I *have* to accept that I might be here for ever."

I started to explore my island. I first went to the little inlet where I had brought in my raft from the ship. I followed it for two miles until I came to a stream of fresh, clear water. Beyond, at the top of a hill, I found tobacco plants growing, and many other plants whose name I did not know. Soon, I came to thick woods and found them full of melons and ripe grapes.

"Perhaps I should move here," I thought to myself, "it is safe from storms. But no," I decided, "I must be near the seashore to watch for passing ships. I will put a little tent here, and I can stay whenever I want."

I spent a night in these woods, the first time I had dared to stay away from my fort. I slept in a tree! As I walked on the next day, past trees bearing cocoa, oranges, limes and lemons, a feeling of great pride came over me. I was lord and king of *all* this country.

Some weeks after this short exploration, I made up my

mind to travel around the whole island. I found the other side of the island was much pleasanter. It was full of grass and flowers, goats and brightly coloured parrots. After my travels, I realised that I had begun to think differently. I had a future on the island. No longer did I feel a prisoner. No longer did I sit and weep for hours on end.

"It is possible for me to be happy alone," I said to myself, "and even happier than I have been anywhere else in my life."

I almost thanked God for bringing me to this place; but I stopped myself. That would not be right. After all, I still hoped that somebody would rescue me. Instead, I thanked God for opening my eyes and for letting me see life in a new way.

And with these thoughts, I began my fourth year on the island. I had often thought of trying to reach the mainland. I tried to move my boat but it was too heavy. Then I started to make a small canoe.

How strange I must have looked by then! I saved all the skins from the animals I killed and dried them. I made a great cap for my head, with the hair on the outside to keep off the rain. This worked so well that I made clothes and shoes in the same way. I spent many weeks making an umbrella like the ones I had seen in Brazil. Now I could walk out in the hottest and wettest weather.

It was two more years before I had finished my canoe and dragged it into the water. I put a large tortoise and a jar of fresh water on board and pushed away from the shore. Suddenly, the current began to carry me out to sea.

"O happy island!" I cried out, "I shall never see you again!"

We do not appreciate what we have until it is taken away from us. I prayed that the current would bring me back again to shore, and it did.

I gave up all thoughts of ever trying to escape again from the island.

I lived happily for another six years with my animals and my parrot, Poll, who talked to me all day long.

★　★　★　★　★

One day, everything changed. I found the print of a man's bare foot in the sand!

I stood still by the sea, frozen with fear for a moment. The man's footprint was very clear. I listened, I looked round me. I could see nothing, I could hear nothing. I walked up and down the shore. I could see only that footprint.

I ran straight home to my fortress. I was terrified all the time, looking behind me at every two or three steps, mistaking every bush or tree for a man. And when I came to my castle, as I called it from this day, I fled inside like a man who is chased by wild animals. Never has a fox run to earth as quickly as I did that day.

I did not sleep at all that night. Questions spun round in my head.

Why was there only one footprint? Where was the ship that had brought the man? Why should anyone want to come to my island after all these years?

After much thought, I made my decision.

"This footprint must be that of one of the men who live on the mainland," I said to myself. "The wind or the strong current have brought his canoe here."

Then, with a sinking heart, I remembered my own canoe.

"What if they have found it?" I cried in torment. "They might come back with more of their people to eat me! And even if they do not find me, they might find my animals and my food and eat it. Then I would die anyway."

I was filled with fear again, as I had been when I first came to the island. Once I had trembled with fear because I was alone. But now I trembled at the sight of a man's footprint!

"Perhaps I have made a mistake," I told myself. "Perhaps the footprint is my own!"

This thought cheered me up a little. I even went outside to milk my goats. I saw nothing, and although I was still afraid, I became braver.

"I will go back to the seashore," I thought, "and measure the footprint against my own."

I went there straight away, looking behind me all the time. I put my foot in the footprint and stared in surprise. The footprint in the sand was much larger than mine! I shook with fear and ran straight back home.

For the next few years, I did everything I could to make my home more secure. I planted trees around it so that no man might get through. I divided my flock of goats and kept six on three different pieces of land. All that hard work, just because of one footprint on the sand!

Then I came across a sight far more terrifying than the footprint.

CHAPTER FIVE

Bones on the sand

In the following years, I travelled around the whole island many times, always searching for secret places where I could hide my animals. One day, I went further west than usual and climbed down to the seashore. Suddenly, I stopped in surprise. There in front of me on the sand was a human skull, and the bones of human hands and feet. Nearby were the remains of a fire and smooth sand all around it.

I was so astonished by this sight that I forgot that I might be in danger.

"I have often heard about people who eat their fellow men," I cried out, "but I have never seen it with my own eyes!"

I turned away and I was sick on the sand. I could not bear to stay in the place any longer and I walked back home as quickly as I could. How could I have not realised it before? The cannibals often fought their enemies in canoes. Why should they not bring their victims to the island to kill and eat them?

"Thank you, God, " I cried at last, "for bringing me that stormy day to the side of the island where these cannibals never came."

I calmed myself with one other thought.

"These men never come to the island looking for people to eat," I told myself, "they bring their victims with them."

But the discovery of the bones shocked and saddened me. I kept to my own territory for almost two years afterwards. I hardly ever fired my gun, in case one of the cannibals heard it, and I relied on my goats for food and milk.

I chose a place on the hill where I might be able to watch for the men arriving in their canoes.

"Then I can wait for them in the trees by the shore and shoot them before they could carry out their terrible crime," I thought.

And every day, I climbed to the top of the hill to watch for boats. As long as I had this plan in my head, I felt quite safe, especially as I never saw any boats.

One day, a new thought came into my mind

"What right had *I* to kill these men? God has not punished them so far. Perhaps they do not see what they do as a crime? They eat men as we eat animals!"

I gave up my plans to attack them.

"I shall make sure they do not see me, and I shall leave them in peace," I decided.

I did not leave my home so much in the following year, my twenty-third on the island. By now, my parrot Poll could speak to me, and he amused me a great deal. When I did go out to milk my goats, my imagination sometimes got the better of me. What would I do if I suddenly met twenty or more cannibals with bows and arrows?

The constant danger I was in changed the way I lived my life. I cared now more for my safety than my food. I moved my fire deep into a cave, which I found by chance when I was gathering firewood. This cave was so dry and secret that I moved my spare guns and gunpowder there, too.

"I am like one of those giants in a story who always lives in a cave where no one can reach him," I laughed to myself. "Even if five hundred cannibals were to hunt me, they could never find me out; or, if they did, they would not try to attack me here."

A few months later, I saw a fire on the seashore on *my*

side of the island. It was December, the month when I harvested my crops. I had set off for my fields very early in the morning, even before it was completely light. In the early dawn, I saw firelight about two miles away.

I was shocked at the sight after so many years. I dared not go any further. I went straight back to my fortress and pulled up the ladder. I loaded all my guns and placed them on the walls. When I grew tired of waiting, I crept up the hill with my looking-glass. I laid down flat and looked for the fire.

Soon, I caught sight of nine men sitting round a small fire they had made, not to warm them, but to eat the human flesh they had brought with them. I did not know whether it was alive or dead. There were two canoes at the edge of the water.

It was shocking to see these men so close to me.

As soon as they had left, I put two guns over my shoulders, and a pistol in each hand. I made my way down to the shore. Once again, I stared at the blood and bones and the flesh of human bodies. And once again, I wanted to kill the men who had done it. My great anxiety returned.

Every day, I expected to fall into the hands of these wild creatures.

CHAPTER SIX

Man Friday

Three years passed by. I had almost stopped dreaming about the cannibals when, early one morning, I saw no less than five empty canoes on my side of the island.

"Where have they gone?" I wondered, "there must be at least thirty of them."

I got my guns ready at my castle and waited for an attack; but none came. I climbed the hill with my spyglass and looked down at the shore. There were at least thirty men dancing around their fire.

As I watched, I saw two miserable prisoners being dragged from one of the canoes. One of them was hit with a spear and fell to the ground. Three cannibals immediately cut him up ready for their cookery.

The other victim stood still for a moment, watching. Then he seized his chance and ran with amazing speed in the direction of my home. I was terrified.

"Now my nightmare will come true!" I gasped. "The others will follow him. They will discover me."

I felt happier when I saw that only two or three men ran after him, and soon they lost him because he ran so swiftly. Suddenly, a thought came to me.

"This man might be a companion for me, or a servant.

I must save his life."

I ran as fast as I could towards the victim and placed myself between him and his attackers.

"Over here!" I shouted to him, "over here."

I ran at the first cannibal and knocked him down. I did not want to shoot at him for fear that the others would hear. The second one raised his bow and drew back the arrow. I had to shoot him to save myself.

Their poor victim was so frightened by the noise and fire of my gun that he stood completely still.

"Come here," I said again, "come here. I shall not hurt you."

He walked a little way, then stopped, trembling as if I had taken him prisoner again and was about to kill him. He came forward again, and knelt every ten or twelve steps to thank me for saving his life. When he reached me, he kissed the ground, lifted my foot and placed it on his head.

As he did this, the man I had knocked to the ground got up. I spoke to the man at my feet and he answered. I could not understand his words, but I thought they were pleasant to hear, for they were the first sound of a man's voice that I had heard for twenty-five years. He pointed to my sword. I gave it to him. With one clean stroke, he cut off the head of the cannibal and placed it at my feet, along with my sword.

I turned to go, pointing towards my cave.

"Come with me," I told him.

He shook his head and pointed to the bodies on the ground, then in the direction of the canoes. I made a digging movement with my hands and he set to work, burying both bodies in fifteen minutes.

Then I took him to my cave.

The young man I had saved was a handsome fellow, tall

and well-shaped. His hair was long and black, his skin olive, his face round and plump. He looked gentle and kind.

"I shall call you Friday," I told him, "for today is Friday. And you shall call me Master."

I taught him to say "yes" and "no" and their meaning. I showed him how to drink milk from a bowl. I gave him clothes to wear. The next day, we went down to the shore to make sure that the cannibals had gone. As we were walking past the buried bodies of the savages, Friday knelt down and dug in the sand. He put his hand to his mouth.

I was horrified.

"No! No!" I shouted, "we do not eat men!"

There was no sign of the cannibals or their canoes. But once again, I gazed in horror at the sight that met my eyes on the beach. My blood ran cold in my veins. The sand was covered with human bones, the ground red with their blood, half eaten and mangled pieces of flesh here and there. I counted three skulls, five hands and the bones of three or four legs and feet.

Friday was not upset at all. In fact, I saw that he would have eaten the flesh if I let him. But he knew that I would kill him if he did such a thing. We set to work and buried the bones in the sand.

I hoped that I would never see such a terrible sight again.

CHAPTER SEVEN
We make a canoe

The next year was the happiest I had spent on the island, thanks to my new companion. I taught him my language. He was quick to learn and so eager to please me that I could have stayed there forever, except for the fear I still had of the cannibals. And at first, I was worried for my own safety when Friday came to live with me because of his liking for human flesh.

"What if he wants to eat me?" I thought. "I must get him used to animal flesh as soon as possible."

I decided to take Friday hunting with me. In the woods, I came across a she-goat with two of her kids.

"Stay there," I whispered to him.

I walked forward, aimed my gun and shot one of the kids. Friday was so afraid that he almost fainted. He had not seen the dead kid yet and he thought that I had shot him. He searched his body for marks of the gunpowder. I laughed, took him by the hand and led him over to the dead kid. I loaded my gun again and shot a bird above us.

I cooked the meat for us and gave some to Friday. He liked it very much. When he promised that he would never eat human flesh again, I was very relieved.

"Well, Friday," I said one evening, "what do your

people do with the men they take prisoner? Do they eat them up?"

"Yes, Master," Friday replied, "my people eat mans too, eat all up."

"Where do they take them?" I asked. "Do they come here?"

"Yes, yes, Master," he said, "they come here."

I hesitated, then spoke again.

"Have you been here with them?" I asked.

"Yes," replied Friday, "I been here."

So my man Friday had been one of the cannibals I had seen from my hill top! I was shocked. But then I asked a very important question.

"How far is it from this island to your country?"

I understood from his answer that he came from an island I knew as Trinidad, and that he belonged to the Carib people. Friday had come to my island safely. Perhaps he could help me to escape to his! I took Friday to see the remains of the boat that had brought me near the shore twenty-six years ago. But the sun had rotted it.

"Friday," I began, "do you wish to go back to your people?"

"Yes," he told me, "very much."

"Would you eat man again there?" I asked.

He shook his head.

"My people learn much from the bearded mans," he

said. "They tell us it is wrong."

I was suddenly excited.

"Friday, how many bearded men are over there?" I asked.

He counted on his fingers. "Fifteen…sixteen… seventeen."

I knew that these men must be Spanish or Portuguese or even my own countrymen.

"How can I go to your island?" I asked.

"In two boats," Friday replied.

"I do not understand," I said.

"A very big boat," Friday said.

From this time, I held on to the idea of leaving the island. I went to work with Friday to cut down a great tree. I showed him how to use my tools and, after a month's hard work, we had finished our canoe. It would have easily carried twenty men.

We pulled the canoe into the water. I was amazed to see how well Friday could turn and move it. We could have set off then, but I wanted to make a mast and sails and a rudder to steer her.

"Now we will wait for November or December," I told him, "then the weather will be good."

One morning in November, I sent Friday down to the beach to collect turtle eggs for our voyage. He came running back, his feet hardly touching the ground.

"O Master!" he cried, "O sorrow! O bad!"

With a trembling hand, he pointed out to sea.

CHAPTER EIGHT

We fight the cannibals

"What's the matter, Friday?" I asked.

"There! Over there!" he said, "one, two, three canoe! One, two, three!"

"Do not be frightened," I said. "We will fight them. Can you fight, Friday?"

"Me shoot," he replied, "but there come many great number."

I set off up the hill with my spy-glass. I discovered quickly that there were twenty-one cannibals, three prisoners and three canoes. They had come to feast.

"We shall kill them all," I shouted to Friday, sick at heart, "will you fight with me?"

Friday nodded.

I gave him some guns and we set out.

"Keep close behind me," I told him, "and do not shoot until I tell you."

Was I doing the right thing? These people had done me no harm. Should I leave it to God to punish them?

"I will go near to them and watch," I told myself, "then I will do as God decides."

It was difficult to stay quiet when we reached the edge of the shore and watched from a little hill about eighty yards away. A terrible sight met our eyes. One of the prisoners was a bearded white man wearing clothes. Two of the cannibals were untying the ropes around his feet.

"Now!" I shouted to Friday. "Fire!"

Friday took his aim much better than I did. He killed two of them and wounded three more. I killed one and wounded two. All those who were not hurt jumped to their feet, not knowing where to run. We fired again. Many of them fell to the ground, wounded.

"Follow me, Friday!" I shouted.

I rushed out of the wood and showed myself. Friday came after me, and we shouted and screamed loudly. We shot the other cannibals, some of them already in the canoes. I untied the ropes of their victim, and spoke to him in Portuguese. He was so weak that he could hardly speak.

"Where are you from?" I asked again, in English.

He made me understand that he was Spanish.

"We will talk later," I told him, "but if you have any strength left, take this pistol and sword, and fight!"

He took the weapons and cut two of his murderers to pieces. After a long fight, we had killed seventeen cannibals and four had escaped in their canoe.

"Follow me, Friday!" I shouted. "We must follow them, or they will bring back hundreds of men to kill us."

I jumped into one of the canoes and, to my surprise, found another poor prisoner there - alive, tied hand and foot, but almost dead with fear. I cut him free, but he groaned in terror.

"Friday," I called, "tell this man that he is safe. We do not wish to kill him."

Friday came over to the man. Then he hugged him, and laughed and cried, danced and sang. I watched in astonishment.

"This man is my father," he told me at last.

I was happy for my friend; but it meant that we could not follow the cannibals.

"Do you think they will come back to kill us?" I asked Friday.

He shook his head. "The wind blows hard," he said, "they drown. If they live, they much afraid of guns."

I tried not to worry any more.

CHAPTER NINE

Mutiny at sea

There were now four people on my island.

"They all owe their lives to me," I thought, "and I feel like a real king because they all obey me!"

I began to think again of going to Friday's island. His father told me that I would be well treated. I talked to the Spaniard about my plans, and asked him about the bearded men.

"Yes, there are sixteen of my fellow men still over there," he told me. "We swam ashore when our ship sank."

"Did you ever try to escape?" I asked him.

"We often talked about it," he said, "but we had no boat and no tools to make one."

"You could bring your friends over here," I said. "I have a boat big enough for twenty men. But can I trust them? The English and the Spanish are enemies."

"You can trust them," he said seriously. "You have saved my life."

"Then you and Friday's father should set out as soon as possible to bring them back," I said.

"There will not be enough food for us all now," he replied. "Why don't we sow more seeds and fetch them

41

after the harvest?"

"You are right," I said, "and we shall start work today."

We went freely around the island to sow our crops, no longer fearing the cannibals now there were four of us with guns. A few months later, we took in a good harvest. Friday's father and the Spaniard set off at last for the mainland. They had only been gone eight days when Friday came running to me.

"Master! Master!" he shouted. "They are come, they are come!"

I took my telescope and climbed to the top of a hill.

"These are not the people we are expecting, Friday!" I called. "It is an English ship. Something is wrong, I know it!"

I watched carefully. A small boat came towards the shore. I could see eleven sailors on board; but, to my surprise, three of them were tied up with rope.

"O Master!" cried Friday, "you see English man eat prisoner."

"No, no," I replied, "I am afraid they will murder them, Friday. They will not eat them."

The sailors left their prisoners in the shade of a tree and went into the woods to sleep. Friday and I, carrying as many guns as we could, crept towards the prisoners. Then I walked over to them. They stared at me in astonishment.

"Gentlemen, do not be surprised at me," I said, "I am your friend."

"Are you a real man or an angel?" wept one of the men.

"If God had sent an angel, he would have been better clothed!" I laughed.

The man told me his story and I believed him. He was the captain of the ship out in the bay. Some of the sailors had taken over his ship and planned to leave him, and his two men, on the island.

"If we help you to take back your ship, will you take me and my man back to England?" I asked.

"Of course," said the captain, "for I shall owe my life to you."

"I can hardly believe it!" I gasped. "After almost thirty years, I can leave this island."

And I wept.

Chapter Ten

Escape from my island

As we spoke, we heard the voices of the mutineers. I gave the men guns and we waited. The captain shot two of the men when they came out of the trees and the rest surrendered straight away. We made a hole in their small boat in case the mutineers tried to get back to the ship.

Soon, another boat came from the ship to look for the men. Three of this search party stayed with the boat on the shore and the other seven began to make their way inland. I was disappointed.

"We must attack the men in the boat when their mates are out of sight," I said, "or they will go back to the ship and say there is trouble. I don't want the ship to sail without us."

The mutineers stopped at the edge of the wood, afraid. I sent Friday to a small hill and he shouted until the sailors moved forward again. The rest of us attacked the men in the boat and took them prisoner.

Night was beginning to fall. The other mutineers made their way slowly back to the boat. When they found the men had gone, they shouted their names. We crept forward.

"That's the man who led the mutiny! He mustn't

escape," whispered the captain.

He shot the man dead.

"They cannot see how few we are," I said.

"Here's our captain with fifty men," called out one of the captain's men.

The terrified mutineers surrendered on the spot.

"Now I must get back my ship," said the captain. "I shall fire seven guns when we have taken her."

I climbed a hill overlooking the bay and waited. The silence was heavy. Just when I could hardly bear it any longer, at about two o'clock in the morning, I heard the guns. I lay down on the grass and went to sleep.

The captain's voice woke me up.

"My dear friend," he said, pointing across the bay, "there's your ship, for she is all yours."

I looked out to sea and there she was, only half a mile from the shore, and her small boat waiting where I had first landed my raft. I almost fainted on the ground and I could not speak. When I was stronger, I knelt down and thanked God for his help.

The captain had brought me fine clothes to wear. I put them on and he paraded his prisoners in front of me.

"I am the Governor of this island," I told them. "I can decide whether you go back to England to be hanged or whether I let you stay here."

I stared at them.

"Could you live here, as I have done all these years?"
I asked.

After a while, they nodded and muttered their thanks.
And then I told them how I had lived on the island, how
I had kept my animals and grown my crops. I told them
every part of my story.

I left my island the next day, on 19 December, 1686,
after twenty-eight years, two months and nineteen days.
I left everything behind for the mutineers, except for my
umbrella, my goatskin hat, my money, my parrot – and
my man Friday.

★   ★   ★   ★   ★

I married when I returned to England and had two
sons and a daughter. My old friends in Brazil had sold my
farm and the money I received allowed me to live well.

After my wife's death, I decided to visit my Caribbean
island again. It had changed a great deal. The Spaniard's
friends had moved there from the mainland; but there
was often trouble between them and mutineers. I gave
them a part of the island each before I left.

I never settled down again. I went to sea many times
– and Friday was always my faithful companion.

Glossary

Key:

adj	adjective
adv	adverb
n	noun
phr	phrase
phr v	phrasal verb
(superl)	superlative
vi	intransitive verb
vt	transitive verb

angel	*n*	a type of good spirit	43
bankrupt	*adj*	if you are bankrupt, you don't have enough money to pay your debts	5
be hanged, to	*passive*	to be killed by having a rope tied around your neck then being left to swing, for example, from a tree	45
bow and arrow	*n*	an arrow is like a short spear; a bow is used to shoot arrows	27
cabin	*n*	a small room on a ship	7
cannibal	*n*	a person who eats the flesh of other people	7
carpenter	*n*	a person who makes and repairs things made of wood	12
cellar	*n*	a room in the bottom of a house, which is under the ground	13
current	*n*	a flowing movement in the sea or in a river	21

despair	*n*	the opposite of hope	18
eager to...	*phr*	wanting very much to...	34
earthquake	*n*	when the earth shakes	15
fall into the hands of, to	*phr*	to be captured by	28
feast, to	*vi*	to have a big meal	38
fellow sailor	*n*	if you are a sailor, the other sailors you are with are your fellow sailors	10
flesh	*n*	the soft parts of your body; meat	33
for the fear that...	*phr*	in case...	31
fort	*n*	a strong building in which you are protected from your enemies	19
froth	*n*	lots of white bubbles	15
get the better of, to	*phr*	if something gets the better of you, it becomes too strong for you to resist	27
guilt	*n*	the bad feeling you get when you know you have done something wrong and you regret it	18
hammock	*n*	a piece of material used as a bed by hanging it between trees or poles, for example	12
harvest, to	*vt*	to cut down or pick plants for food	28
herd	*n*	a group of animals, such as cattle or goats, that live together	24
high tide	*n*	the time at which the sea is at its highest	11

50

hurricane	*n*	a type of violent wind storm	15
in torment	*phr*	in a very worried way	23
inlet	*n*	a long, narrow bit of sea almost surrounded by land	19
kid	*n*	a young goat	34
looking-glass *(old fashioned)*	*n* *(here)*	a small telescope	28
mainland	*n*	a large area of land, as opposed to the islands around it	23
mangled	*adj*	if something is mangled, it is so badly damaged that you can't see what it originally looked like	33
mast	*n*	a tall pole on a boat, to which sails are attached	11
mate	*n* *(here)*	a fellow sailor	44
mouth (of a river)	*n*	where a river meets the sea	7
mutiny	*n*	if there is a mutiny on a ship, the sailors refuse to obey their captain	41
on board	*phr*	if you climb on board, you climb onto a ship or boat	8
on the spot	*phr*	immediately	45
parade (prisoners), to	*vt*	to show your prisoners by making them walk in procession	45
parrot	*n*	a kind of exotic bird that people sometimes keep as a pet	20

Plague, the	*n*	a very serious disease that generally causes death	5
plump	*adj*	fat	33
prowling	*adj*	moving quietly, for example when hunting	12
quarrel	*n*	a serious disagreement	5
rely on, to	*phr*	to need or depend on something for a particular purpose	26
rudder	*n*	a long piece of metal or wood at the back of a boat; the rudder goes into the water and is used for steering	37
run to earth, to	*phr*	to run and hide in the ground	23
sandbank	*n*	an area of sand just below the surface of the sea	8
search party	*n*	a group of people who are looking for someone	44
seashore	*n*	the edge of the sea; a beach	11
shipwreck	*n*	an accident at sea that destroys a ship	7
shriek, to	*vt*	to shout	8
sick at heart	*adj*	very upset	38
sinking: with a sinking heart	*phr*	feeling depressed or worried	23
spear	*n*	a weapon made from a long, thin piece of wood with a sharp metal point at the end	16

spy	*n*	a person who collects secret information for a government or organisation	5
stay afloat, to	*phr*	if something stays afloat, it does not sink	8
steer (a boat), to	*vt*	to control the direction that a boat is travelling in	37
struggle to one's feet, to	*phr*	to stand up, with difficulty	8
surrender, to	*vi*	to stop fighting because you agree that your opponent is stronger than you	44
swallow something up, to	*phr*	if something swallows you up, you disappear completely into it	7
sword	*n*	a kind of long knife used as a weapon	32
tea chest	*n*	a large box used for transporting tea	18
telescope	*n*	a long instrument used to see things that are far away	42
tortoise	*n*	an animal that has a hard, rounded shell	21
trade, to	*vi*	to buy and sell things	7
turtle	*n*	a sea creature similar to a tortoise	37
uproot (a tree), to	*vt*	to knock a tree down so that its roots come out of the ground	15
vein	*n*	a tube that carries blood in your body	33
voyage	*n*	a journey by sea	37
wound, to	*vt*	to injure	39

Robinson Crusoe Test Yourself

Exercise 1

Write a number to complete each sentence.

1 Crusoe was _____ years old when he
   ran away from home.

2 He left the tobacco farm in Brazil _____ years later.

3 The first storm lasted _____ days.

4 There were _____ men on the boat.

5 He arrived on the island on the _____ September, 1659.

6 The earthquake lasted at least _____ minutes.

7 He spent _____ days and nights in the cave after
   the hurricane.

8 It took him _____ years to make his canoe.

9 He found _____ footprint in the sand.

10 In his twenty-third year on the island, he saw a group
   of _____ cannibals for the first time.

Exercise 2

Are these sentences true (T) or false (F)?

1 Friday was horrified to see the bones and blood on the beach.

2 When Friday first escaped from the cannibals, Crusoe was very happy.

3 Friday did not like eating goat.

4 Friday had visited the island before.

5 The bearded victim of the cannibals was Spanish.

6 Five cannibals escaped from Crusoe.

7 Friday's father and the Spaniard came back from the mainland after eight days.

8 The captain of the ship had been made a prisoner by some of the sailors.

9 The captain killed the man who had led the mutiny.

10 Crusoe and Friday continued to travel after they left the island.

Answers

Exercise 1	1 eighteen;
	2 nine;
	3 twelve;
	4 eleven;
	5 30th;
	6 thirty;
	7 two;
	8 two;
	9 one;
	10 nine

Exercise 2	1 F; 2 F; 3 F; 4 T; 5 T; 6 F; 7 F; 8 T; 9 T; 10 T